MW01138602

Cultural Celebrations

DAY OF THE DEAD

DiscoverRoo
An Imprint of Pop!
popbooksonline.com

Patricia Hutchison

abdobooks.com

Published by Pop!, a division of ABDO, PO Box 398166, Minneapolis, Minnesota 55439. Copyright © 2021 by POP, LLC. International copyrights reserved in all countries. No part of this book may be reproduced in any form without written permission from the publisher. Pop!™ is a trademark and logo of POP, LLC.

Printed in the United States of America, North Mankato, Minnesota.

052020
092020

THIS BOOK CONTAINS RECYCLED MATERIALS

Cover Photo: Shutterstock Images
Interior Photos: Shutterstock Images, 1, 5, 6, 8–9, 12, 13, 16 (bottom), 17 (top), 17 (bottom), 23 (ofrenda), 23 (photo), 24–25, 28, 30; Ronen Tivony/Sipa USA/AP Images, 7; Archiv Gerstenberg/ullstein bild Dtl./Getty Images, 11; Werner Forman/Universal Images Group/Getty Images, 14; olneystudio/Alamy, 15; iStockphoto, 16 (top), 19, 21, 22, 26; El Universal/Iván Stephens/RCC/GDA/AP Images, 20; Cristopher Rogel Blanquet/Getty Images News/Getty Images, 27, 31; Karel Navarro/AP Images, 29

Editor: Connor Stratton
Series Designer: Jake Slavik

Content Consultant: Elizabeth C. Martinez, PhD, Professor of Latin American and Latino Studies, DePaul University

Library of Congress Control Number: 2019955003
Publisher's Cataloging-in-Publication Data

Names: Hutchison, Patricia, author.

Title: Day of the dead / by Patricia Hutchison

Description: Minneapolis, Minnesota : POP!, 2021 | Series: Cultural celebrations | Includes online resources and index

Identifiers: ISBN 9781532167683 (lib. bdg.) | ISBN 9781532168789 (ebook)

Subjects: LCSH: Day of the Dead--Juvenile literature. | All Souls' Day--Juvenile literature. | Holidays--Juvenile literature. | Social customs--Juvenile literature.

Classification: DDC 394.266--dc23

WELCOME TO DiscoverRoo!

Pop open this book and you'll find QR codes loaded with information, so you can learn even more!

Scan this code* and others like it while you read, or visit the website below to make this book pop!

popbooksonline.com/day-of-the-dead

*Scanning QR codes requires a web-enabled smart device with a QR code reader app and a camera.

TABLE OF
CONTENTS

CHAPTER 1
CELEBRATING LIFE

On November 1 and 2, skeletons fill the

streets. But they are not meant to be

scary. Instead, they dance and wear

bright colors. Day of the Dead is like a

WATCH A
VIDEO HERE!

Millions of people attend the Day of the Dead parade in Mexico City every year.

lively family **reunion**. People honor family members who have died.

Many people put on skeleton makeup to celebrate Day of the Dead.

Day of the Dead is celebrated in

Mexico. On this holiday, some people

believe that **departed** loved ones return

to Earth. The dead do not want to find their friends and families sad. Instead, they expect to see parties.

Some Latino Americans celebrate Day of the Dead in the United States.

Day of the Dead celebrates life. Decorations line the streets. People dance. They play fun music. The holiday treats death as a normal part of life.

In Spanish, Day of the Dead is known as Día de los Muertos.

DID YOU KNOW?

People hold many beliefs about Day of the Dead. Some people think the border between the real world and the spirit world disappears.

CHAPTER 2
HISTORY OF DAY OF THE DEAD

For hundreds of years, the Aztecs ruled much of present-day Mexico. These people believed the dead had to make a final journey. The trip was long and hard. So, families left food and tools for their

LEARN MORE HERE!

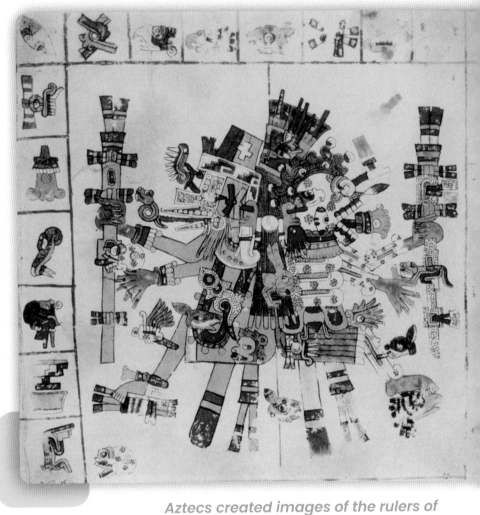

Aztecs created images of the rulers of Mictlan, the dead's final resting place.

loved ones. These items would help make

the journey easier for the dead.

Putting candles by graves is one practice of All Souls' Day.

In the 1500s, the Spanish took over

Mexico. Most people from Spain were

Catholic. They celebrated All Saints'

Day and All Souls' Day. These feasts

happened on November 1 and 2.

For All Saints' Day, people often put flowers by loved ones' graves.

DID YOU KNOW?

Catholic holidays often mixed with pre-Christian holidays, such as a fall celebration known as Samhain. People had feasts for the dead.

The Spanish forced most Aztecs to become Catholic. But the Aztecs kept many of their **traditions**. On November 1, for example, they celebrated **departed** children.

Aztecs made sculptures of the god Mictlantecuhtli, who ruled over Mictlan.

Nahuatl is a language related to what Aztecs spoke. Approximately 1.5 million people speak that language today.

On November 2, people honored adults who had passed away. These traditions have lived on over hundreds of years.

CELEBRATING DAY OF THE DEAD

OCTOBER 31

People decorate the graves of young children. Many believe that these souls rise at midnight.

NOVEMBER 1

After being with their families, the children's souls return to the land of the dead. Then the adults' spirits arrive. These spirits arrive in the form of butterflies.

NOVEMBER 3

In some places, actors wearing masks run around town. They chase souls back to the land of the dead. Families blow out the candles and take down the decorations.

NOVEMBER 2

Families eat a dinner that includes Day of the Dead bread. Some families set a place at the table for their departed loved one. Families also visit and decorate their loved one's grave.

CHAPTER 3

BUILDING AN OFRENDA

For Day of the Dead, most families build ofrendas in their homes. These **altars** honor loved ones who have died. A **traditional** ofrenda has certain items.

COMPLETE AN ACTIVITY HERE!

Paper banners hang above the ofrenda. They represent the element of wind.

People set out food and water for the spirits. They light candles too. These items are **symbols** of Earth, water, and fire.

A picture of a loved one sits framed on the ofrenda.

Each ofrenda is different. But a family

often places pictures on top of the altar.

These pictures show **departed** loved

ones. People may also scatter jewelry

and clothing on the altar. They often put

out marigolds too.

MARIGOLDS

Marigold petals are often an important part of ofrendas. Their strong scent attracts departed loved ones. It helps them find their way to the food on the altars. The bright flowers also show the beauty of life. The orange and yellow colors remind people of the sun. They are symbols of rebirth. In the Nahuatl language, marigolds are called *cempasuchil*.

A family also puts Day of the Dead bread on the altar. This bread tends to be sweet. It may have strips of bread that are laid on top. The strips represent bones.

In Spanish, the holiday's bread is known as pan de muerto.

PARTS OF AN OFRENDA

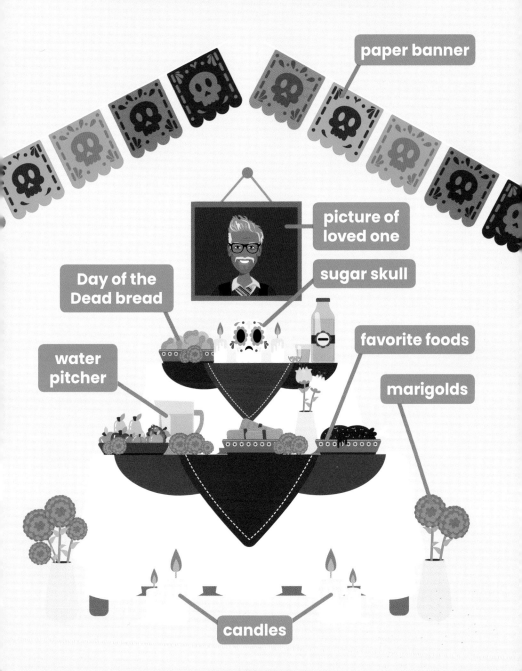

paper banner

picture of loved one

sugar skull

Day of the Dead bread

favorite foods

water pitcher

marigolds

candles

CHAPTER 4
SYMBOLS AND GRAVESIDE PARTIES

Day of the Dead has many **symbols**.

Skulls and skeletons are some main

ones. Sweet sugar

skulls decorate

the ofrenda.

People wear skull-shaped

masks in the parade.

The skulls are colorful.

Many have big smiles.

They show how death

is another part of life.

LEARN MORE HERE!

Monarch butterflies are also important symbols. Every fall, the butterflies travel to Mexico for the winter. Aztecs believed these butterflies were the spirits of their dead **ancestors**. Today, people visit the places where the butterflies land.

monarch butterfly

During Day of the Dead parades, some people dress up like skeleton monarch butterflies.

During graveside parties, family members sing, dance, and eat. They share stories about their loved ones.

On November 2, families travel to the cemetery. They clean their loved ones' graves. They decorate the graves too. Then the families throw parties at the cemetery. Every family celebrates Day of the Dead differently. But the holiday helps them remember and honor their loved ones.

Musicians play at a grave during Day of the Dead.

MAKING CONNECTIONS

TEXT-TO-SELF

Do you find skeletons scary? Why or why not?

TEXT-TO-TEXT

Have you read books about other holidays that people celebrate? What do they have in common with Day of the Dead? How are they different?

TEXT-TO-WORLD

Skulls and skeletons are some of the symbols of Day of the Dead. What is one holiday you celebrate? What are some common symbols of that holiday?

GLOSSARY

altar – a raised table where offerings are placed.

ancestor – a family member who lived long ago.

departed – no longer alive.

reunion – a gathering of people who have been apart.

symbol – something that stands for something else because of certain similarities.

tradition – a belief or way of doing things that is passed down from person to person over time.

INDEX

ONLINE RESOURCES

popbooksonline.com

Scan this code* and others
like it while you read, or visit
the website below to make
this book pop!

popbooksonline.com/day-of-the-dead

*Scanning QR codes requires a web-enabled smart device with a QR code reader app and a camera.